THE COUSINS THREE

MEET THE COUSINS THREE

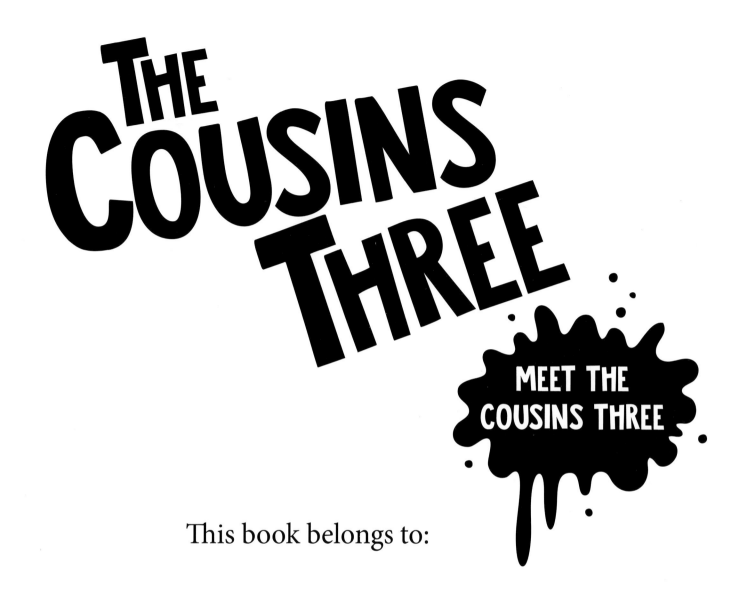

This book belongs to:

_____

WRITTEN BY:

AMY LAURA LEISTEN

ILLUSTRATED BY:

LUIGI A. CANNAVICCI

Published by Bright Finch Books 2019
ISBN: 978-1-7339536-0-3
Copyright © 2021 by Amy Leisten
Written by Amy Leisten
Cover and internal illustrations by Luigi Cannavicci

Printed in the United States of America

www.brightfinchbooks.com

To my wonderful nephews and niece:
Christian, Morrison and Gracie-Grace,
the "real" Cousins Three! You have been the very best
inspiration, I dedicate this book to you.

Bo is wearing red. Matu's in blue,
and the girl is Bea in a pink tutu.
they are family, happy as can be.
cousins are the first friends of
you and me!

They love to share their favorite things.
Oh, the happiness this brings!
Let's read about all of them, shall we?
The sharing and so cheerful Cousins Three.

Bo, the oldest loves to race cars.
He Imagines a track of candy bars.
It's fun to race with Matu and Bea,
even during a tea party!

Racing over imaginary sweets,
each hoping to win as they compete.
Speeding around and sipping tea:
So much fun they have, these three!

Bo loves baseball. His Favorite color's Red.
One time at bat, his ball hit a shed.
"It's still a home run!" yelled Matu and Bea,
as Bo slid into home base on one knee!

Cheers **roared** from the massive crowd.
His best best **friends** were Oh-so proud.
With this last home run they **won**,
baseball can be **oodles of fun!**

One more thing: Bo's favorite food is pickles.
He gulps them down on his bicycle.
He shares his treats riding with Matu and Bea,
dropping a few in the trails through the trees.

They saw a monkey way up high.
He jumped down and ran right by,
picking up pickles as they fell to the ground,
crunch, crunch, he ate all that he found.

Now, about **Matu**, the **boy** in **blue**.
He **loves** to **sing** and play **guitar**, too,
even at the **park** while on the **swings**
with **Bo** and **Bea**, who take turns to **sing!**

Playing the guitar and singing with glee,
from the swings to the slide, they all flee,
singing loud, as they slide down and laugh,
down the big slide that looks like a giraffe.

Matu loves **ball.** His favorite color's **blue.**
Oops! He's down to only one **shoe.**
One shoe **less,** he **runs** across the court,
Hoping to **score** and not fall short.

He makes a **basket** for the team.
The **crowd** begins to shout and **scream.**
They **whistle** and yell out, **"woo-hoo!**
Not bad for a **boy** in just one **shoe!"**

One more **thing**: his favorite food is **cake**.
It's **enjoyed** best in a **boat** on a lake.
He **loves** to share his cake with **Bo** and **Bea**
while **rowing** around yelling,
"Here fishy, fishy!"

They spent the whole day out on the water.
Instead of catching fish, all they saw was an otter!
They still had fun, rowing about,
catching sunrays instead of trout!

Don't forget Bea, the last to be born,
whose favorite animal is a unicorn.
Even when they all must go straight to bed,
She gallops around with her cousins instead.
They pretend they have superpowers
as they fly off to planet Mars.
Bea leads them around the room.
Off to planet Mars, they zoom.

Bea loves to dance.
Her favorite color's pink.
Grooving with pals is great,
don't you think?

They **pretend** to dance to **faraway lands,** **twirling** for **kings** and **Queens** holding hands

Bea's favorite food is mac and cheese, eating it even while on a trapeze.

She loves to take her meals up high, while Bo and Matu watch her fly through the sky.

Bo, Matu and Bea are best friends, you see.
We have learned so much about these Cousins Three:

Best friends to sing with while playing guitar,
best friends for unicorn-riding to Mars!

Cousins are the first best friends you meet.
Cousins just really can't be beat!

Now that you've read about Bo, Matu and Bea,
stay tuned for more with the Cousins Three.